minedition
published by Penguin Young Readers Group

Text and Illustrations copyright © 2007 by Ayano Imai
Original title: Chappi
English text adaption by Kathryn Bishop
Coproduction with Michael Neugebauer Publishing Ltd., Hong Kong.
Rights arranged with "minedition" Rights and Licensing AG, Zurich, Switzerland.

Published simultaneously in Canada.
Manufactured in China by Wide World Ltd.
Typesetting in Papyrus
Color separation by Fotoreproduzioni Grafiche, Verona, Italy.

Library of Congress Cataloging-in-Publication Data available upon request.

ISBN 978-0-698-40062-7

10 9 8 7 6 5 4 3 2 1
First Impression

For more information please visit our website: www.minedition.com

CHESTER

Ayano Imai

minedition

Chester lived with a family of three.
They had once been very happy.
But lately the family was always busy with work and school.
They seldom had time for Chester.
He began to feel invisible and unwanted,
and this made him very sad.

One day, the family forgot to take Chester for his walk.
It wasn't the first time, either.
"There must be a better place for me to live," he said.
"I want a home where I won't be forgotten."
Though it broke his heart, Chester set out to find himself a new home.

Chester walked and walked.
He walked so far that he soon found himself at the edge
of the forest, far from the town.
Inside, Chester could hear animals scurrying and playing.
"My goodness, whoever lives here sounds awfully happy,"
Chester said.
"Perhaps this would be a good place for me to live."

But the birds didn't make Chester feel very welcome.

"We don't want a scary wolf living near us!" the birds cried.

"But I'm not a wolf," said Chester. "I'm a dog."

"It doesn't matter. It's too crowded as it is," they said.

So Chester sighed and set off again.

"Maybe the city is the place for me," Chester said.
"I've heard it's very big. Surely there's a home for me there."
   The city was indeed quite large,
   but Chester couldn't find anyone anywhere who might be willing
   to take him in.
   He thought how strange it was that the city could be so big
   yet feel so lonely.

Chester walked throughout the city and was growing extremely tired.

As he looked for a place to rest, he saw that there were price tags everywhere.

"I've never seen so many," Chester said.

"They have so many zeros. It must be expensive to live here or even stop to rest."

But Chester had no money. This was not a place for him.

Just then a very rich lady walked by and asked Chester why he
looked so sad.

"Oh," she said. "You can stay with me.

I've been lonely since I lost my little doggy.

I promise to treat you well!"

So Chester went with her to her house.

It was the biggest house he'd ever seen.

Life there was very luxurious.

He was dressed up in clothes,

and there were all sorts of toys for him to play with.

There were also many servants.

There was even a groomer who brushed him every day.

However, Chester soon grew tired of being treated like
a toy.
He didn't want to be a doll, wearing stiff, uncomfortable clothes.
"I want to be outside," he said. "I want to breathe fresh air
and feel the earth under my paws. I want to be free."
So Chester ran away.

"Oh, this is awful," Chester said.
Outside it had begun to rain.
He felt cold and lonely.
All he wanted was a place to live,
but there didn't seem to be anywhere that was quite right.
He remembered the day he met his family.
Chester was just a puppy.
And it had also been cold and rainy when they found him.
How kind they had been, taking him into their warm house!

Suddenly Chester heard something.

Was he imagining things or were those the voices of his family?

Chester started to bark until he caught sight of them.

Finally, they found each other.

The family had been searching for him ever since he ran away.

"Oh, Chester, we're so sorry! Please come home.

We've missed you so much," they said as they hugged him.

After that day, everything was different.
Chester had found his home.
He was a member of the family
AND
he was taken for walks at least three times a day!